THE AIMER GATE

Robert had a secret place. It was high in the steeple above the chapel clock.

Father had looked after the clock as long as he'd been a smith – but now he was making horseshoes for the war.

Uncle Charlie had come home from the war to help cut the corn harvest. Today was his last day of leave: it was the day that Robert learned about Uncle Charlie's real job: and the day he discovered that his secret place had another secret.

By the same author

THE WEIRDSTONE OF BRISINGAMEN
THE MOON OF GOMRATH
ELIDOR
THE OWL SERVICE
THE STONE BOOK
TOM FOBBLE'S DAY
GRANNY REARDUN

For older readers

RED SHIFT

THE
AIMER GATE

ALAN GARNER

Illustrations by Michael Foreman

FONTANA · LIONS

First published in Great Britain 1978
by William Collins Sons & Co Ltd
First published in Fontana Lions 1979
by William Collins Sons & Co Ltd

© Alan Garner 1978
© Illustrations Michael Foreman 1979
Printed in Great Britain
by Morrison and Gibb

for Simon and Rachel

THE AIMER GATE

Robert took Wicked Winnie off the wall and oiled her.

The sky was coming light. It was going to be a hot day, but now it was cold.

Wicked Winnie was made of oak planks and the frame of a bassinet. Robert had mounted a swivel on the front wheels, and fixed a length of sashcord, so that he could steer her.

He went down the path to the road, set

himself, heeled along twice and put his feet on the bar. The wheels were fast on the hill, and Robert had to lean out at the bottom to take the corner into the lane and over the Moss. The Moss was flat, and when the cart stopped, Robert got off and walked, pulling her after him. He reached Faddock Allman's cottage, and knocked.

"Mister Allman!"

"Who goes there?" shouted Faddock Allman. "Friend or foe?"

"Friend," said Robert.

"Advance, Friend, and be recognised!" said Faddock Allman.

The cottage was on a piece of wet land by the road. Robert went in.

Faddock Allman had swept the floor and tidied his bed. His brew can was by him, his cocoa powder and sugar in two twists of paper.

"Have you had breakfast?" said Robert.

"Ay," said Faddock Allman. "Get on parade."

"You'll need your jacket," said Robert. He helped Faddock Allman put it on. There was a ribbon fastened to the jacket with a safety pin, orange, blue and yellow and a medal hung at the end.

Faddock Allman picked up his brew can, dropped the twists of cocoa and sugar inside, fitted the lid, took hold of the handle in his teeth, and swung across the floor on his arms and onto the seat of the cart. He put two sacks by him, one to sit on, one for his shoulders in case it rained, and wedged his brew against the side.

"Reach us me Toby," he said.

The pith helmet Faddock Allman always wore was on the bed. Robert gave it to him. It was high-topped, and covered with khaki cloth. Faddock Allman settled it on his head, eased the chinstrap, and was ready.

Robert passed the sashcord over his neck and under his arms and pulled. Wicked Winnie sank her wheels in the ground, but when she came to the road proper she moved without sticking.

"Retreat! Forward! Charge!" shouted Faddock Allman.

Robert left the Moss and went up the Hough, past his own house, to Leah's Hill.

There were two fields of corn, one above the other, on Leah's Hill. At the hedgeside, by the bottom field, was a space where Faddock Allman sat in summer, breaking stone to make road flints.

Faddock Allman folded the sacks on the ground and swung himself down to them. He rubbed his arms. "By heck, youth," he said, "it's a thin wind aback of Polly Norbury's."

"Must I go fetch you a brew?" said Robert.

"Only if the Missis has put the kettle on," said Faddock Allman. "And get me hammers."

Robert ran with the brew and Wicked Winnie the few yards to home. The kettle

was on the fire, and Uncle Charlie was sitting by it, cleaning his rifle.

"Now then, Dick-Richard," he said to Robert.

It was Uncle Charlie's last day of leave. His kitbag and equipment stood smart in a corner. Uncle Charlie was always smart. He shaved morning and night and smelt of soap and had his hair cut every week. He was a lance-corporal in the army and wore a stripe on his sleeve. He was so clean he looked as though he washed with donkey-stone.

But his rifle was cleaner. He cleaned his rifle all the time, rubbing linseed into the wood and fine oil on the metal. Father said Uncle Charlie took his rifle to bed with him.

"Now then, Dick-Richard, what are you at?" said Uncle Charlie.

"Is there a brew for Mister Allman?" said Robert.

"It'll be a bad day when there isn't,"

said Uncle Charlie. "I'll get it."

"I'll fetch his hammers," said Robert.

He ran into the end room of the house. It was full of old things – bolts of dirty silk, tools, grease, iron, nails, screws, grain for the hens and hammers for cutting stone. Father let Faddock Allman use the hammers because they were good for nothing else, but he wouldn't let him have them for his own. They had to come back each night. Father kept everything, even string.

Uncle Charlie had put the cocoa and sugar on the table and filled the brew can with tea.

"Come on, Dick-Richard," he said. "Let's be having you."

He slung his rifle on his shoulder, picked up the brew can and went out. Robert ran after him with Wicked Winnie and the hammers.

Men and women were gathering at Leah's Hill. Ozzie Leah had brought a load for the day; scythes, whetstones, bantspinners, rakes, food and drink. The fields were too steep for the self-binder to reap on. He was going to have the corn cut by hand. And the only men skilled to scythe together in a team were Ozzie and Young Ollie Leah and Uncle Charlie.

Robert had never seen Leah's Hill sown. It was always pasture. But, with the war, even the rough meadows were ploughed now.

"Eh up, Starie Chelevek," Uncle Charlie said to Faddock Allman. "Here's your brew." He poured tea out of the can, using the lid as a cup.

Faddock Allman shuffled round on his sack and took the cup. He drank, sucked his lips and held out the lid for more. "That's the ticket," he said.

"Mark time on this," said Uncle Charlie, "and then we'll see if we can't fetch you a drop of Ozzie's stagger-juice."

Faddock Allman laughed.

"And cop hold of this for us," said Uncle

Charlie. He rattled the bolt of his rifle, opened it, checked that the breech was empty, took off the magazine, put the gun together again and handed it to Faddock Allman.

Faddock Allman shouldered the rifle, saluted, and put it down on the sacking and covered it against dust.

"All in!" shouted Ozzie Leah.

The three men took their scythes and a whetstone each and sharpened the blades, two strokes below the edge, one above. The metal rang like swords and bells.

"Here's your hammers, Mister Allman," said Robert.

"Wait on," said Faddock Allman. "I've not finished me brew."

The men stood in a line, at the field edge, facing the hill, Ozzie on the outside, and began their swing. It was a slow swing, scythes and men like a big clock, back and to, back and to, against the hill they walked. They walked and swung, hips forward, letting the weight cut. It was as if they were walking in a yellow water before them. Each blade came up in time with each blade, at Ozzie's march, for if they ever got out of time the blades would cut flesh and bone.

Behind each man the corn swarf lay like silk in the light of poppies. And the women gathered the swarf by armfuls, spun bants of straw and tied in armfuls into sheaves, stacked sheaves into kivvers. Six sheaves stood to a kivver, and the kivvers must stand till the church bells had rung over them three times. Three weeks to harvest: but first was the getting.

Faddock Allman had finished his brew and was sitting, his hands on his leg stumps, watching the men cut the hill.

"You'll be wanting stones, Mister Allman," said Robert.

"Wait on, wait on," said Faddock Allman.

The three men reached the corner by the

gate to the top field, and pivoted in rhythm on the inside man, Young Ollie Leah. Their line was as straight as soldiers, and when Ozzie was abreast they moved forward along the hill.

"Gorgeous," said Faddock Allman.

"Whet!" shouted Ozzie at the end of a blade swing, and the men stopped and sharpened up, two strokes below, one above; two and one, two and one, like a tune. And then they put the whetstones back in their pockets and began to cut again.

"Right, youth," said Faddock Allman. "I've been waiting to get at that devil all year."

"What?" said Robert.

"Yonder," said Faddock Allman.

"Where?" said Robert.

"Go up past them kivvers," said Faddock Allman, "and just inside top field, against the corn, you'll see a little jackacre of land, by itself."

"I know," said Robert.

"Ay, well, if you have a good feckazing in there, you'll see the best stone for road flints there is in the Hough."

"Right, Mister Allman," said Robert, and pulled Wicked Winnie round into the field and up the hill. The ground between the kivvers was sharp stubble that put a polish on his boot soles. He kept slipping, and the stubble caught his knees.

He reached the gate between the two fields. And beyond it there was a dip and a hump of green, with nettles and a few thistles going to seed. The patch was a bite out of the crop.

Robert opened the gate and went in. The rough pasture hadn't been ploughed and the meadow grass was thick. He could feel hardness ruckled under the ground, but he couldn't reach it.

He chopped with the edge of his heel irons at the biggest lump. He kept kicking. The grass came away in tufts, not strong enough to peel, but snagged with white roots. Robert chopped the roots until he reached sand. In the sand there was a corner of stone. He pulled at it but it didn't move. He stamped on it but it didn't break. He got his hand to it, and wrenched. The stone raggled like a tooth, enough to show between it and its own shape in the ground.

Robert tried to lift it straight out, but his hands wouldn't grip and he fell over. He knelt and scooped the sandy earth away, digging along the stone.

It was a proper stone, worked and dressed, and he had hold of one corner. The sides went away from the squared corner and there was nothing for him to grip. The stone went back into the hill.

Robert tugged sideways again. More space showed, and he felt the stone move. He scooped more sand. The stone was yellow white. Now it wagged but wouldn't come. He felt each swing jolt, and had to stop for breath. The grip was going from his fingers; so he spat on his hands, rubbed them together and tugged straight.

The stone sighed out, and he held it. It was a stone clear as a brick, but bigger.

"What the heck?" said Robert.

Now that the hill was open he could reach inside. There was more stone, all the same yellow white, a lot of it cob-ends of rubble, but every piece true. They came more easily the more he got. If a big piece stuck he took the smaller pieces from around and beneath it. Wicked Winnie was soon filled and she was a weight.

Robert held her at full stretch of the sashcord, using himself as a brake, and let her down the hill to Faddock Allman.

"Whet!" shouted Ozzie.

Every step jarred, and he had to stab at the ground with his heels to hold Wicked Winnie from running away with him. He went down the cleared ground of the swarfs.

Then he slipped. The stubble was too polished. Robert sat down hard and slid.

Wicked Winnie was trying to pull him forwards, but he lay back, holding the sashcord, lay back, pressing his shoulders against the hill, his heels furrowing. He didn't want to be dragged face down through that stubble.

Kivvers were all about him. Robert heaved at the sashcord and rolled his body to steer. And Wicked Winnie swung close but didn't hit. The last kivver went by, and Robert, Wicked Winnie and the stones all landed in the quickthorn hedge.

"Yon's a grand lot," said Faddock Allman.

"Whet!" shouted Ozzie.

Up and down the field Robert went. He had never had such a day. When he got stones for Faddock Allman he had to find them one by one, all sorts, in lanes and hedge cops and at the ends of fields, every kind and size. Now, though, it seemed the hill was giving them to him.

"Is that enough, Mister Allman?" said

Robert. He had made a pile that would last till winter.

"Is it heck as like!" said Faddock Allman. "Raunge the beggars out!" So Robert did.

And the scythes went round the field, cutting a square spiral to the centre. The rows of kivvers grew under the heat of the day.

"Baggin!" shouted Ozzie Leah.

The field stopped. Men and women went to the shaded edge, where food and beer were kept. The scythes were sharpened and laid against trees.

"Eh up, Starie Chelevek! Fancy a wet?" Uncle Charlie had left the others and come down to be with Faddock Allman. He'd brought baggin of bread and onion and cheese and a stone bottle of beer, a full gallon. He crouched on one heel and swigged from the bottle. "And what have you been at, Dick-Richard," he said, "mauling guts out of jackacres?"

"It's all cut stone," said Robert, "same as a quarry bank!"

"It is that," said Faddock Allman. He took the bottle from Uncle Charlie and drank. "See at it!" He hit a finished, squared perfect block and it broke into rough road flints. "Grand," said Faddock Allman.

"What's it doing there?" said Robert.

"Nowt," said Faddock Allman. "Grand!" He split another.

"Are all jackacres cut stone?" said Robert.

"Happen," said Faddock Allman. "Number One! Fire!" He smashed a stone. "Number Two! Fire!" He smashed another.

Uncle Charlie uncovered his rifle and polished the stock. He smiled.

"Number Three!" shouted Faddock Allman.

"Cease firing and get your baggin," said Uncle Charlie.

"Cease firing! Scatter homeward!" shouted Faddock Allman, and bit into an onion, and chewed. He laughed at Robert.

"I was twitting you, youth," he said. "You see, I recollect as how, at one time of day, there was a house stood yonder. And I recollect as how, when they fetched it down, I did enjoy chucking cob-ends through windows."

"All in!" shouted Ozzie.

"It was good," said Faddock Allman, "chucking cob-ends." He pulled the peak of his helmet over his eyes. "Number Three! Fire! Number Four! Fire!" He laughed at the rock.

Robert emptied Wicked Winnie, and went to take Father his baggin.

Father was a smith. He was tinsmith, locksmith and blacksmith: and every Monday morning he wound the chapel clock. But now his time went on making horseshoes for the war.

Robert swept Wicked Winnie clean and

oiled her again. He oiled the hubs specially, with Uncle Charlie's fine oil.

He set her in the middle of the road, at the top of the camber, and eased himself in, holding the sashcord. Wicked Winnie wanted to go, but Robert put his boots down. He took his balance, waited for stillness, and gently lifted his boots, not pushing. Nothing happened. He tried not to twitch. Then Wicked Winnie began to move. Robert sat in a crouch, and steered.

The first part of the road was steep and easy, and Wicked Winnie went fast. At the bottom of the hill the road turned upwards and then down again past Long Croft field and under the wood to Chorley. Robert kept to the top of the camber, crouched as small as Faddock Allman.

At the other end of the wood the road ran to a crest that was so low and long that it could be felt more than seen. This was the worst part. Wicked Winnie lost all her speed, coasted, crept, and reached the top.

And at the top she always stopped. But today there was no wind. Robert had taken Uncle Charlie's fine oil to the hubs, the very best. She was still going. Another yard was all she needed.

Wicked Winnie crept. Her wheels were turning. Robert held his breath. His chest was tight. His tongue stuck to his teeth. But he wouldn't breathe.

His eyes started to see rainbows and his head buzzed. Rainbows round everything; boots, wheels, spokes, hubs. The hubs were still. He looked at the rims. They moved, just moved. There was a noise in his ears like a brook. But he didn't breathe. The hard tyres had flecks on them from the road, and the flecks were still moving. They were moving. They were moving faster. Robert let in a sip of air. Wicked Winnie didn't stop. Robert breathed.

Uncle Charlie's oil had done it.

Now it was a straight run to the smithy: a measured mile from home to the smithy, and Wicked Winnie had broken her record, with Uncle Charlie's oil.

"She did it!" Robert shouted, and sat up. "She did it, she did it, she did it!"

Wicked Winnie rolled along under the chapel clock and across the main road to the smithy and lodged against the kerb. Robert ran into the smithy with Father's baggin.

It was noise at the forge, dark and red. The men were making horseshoes, and the apprentice worked the bellows. It was cutting and snapping, heating, sledging, twisting and breaking. Father wasn't there.

Robert ran out again. He pulled Wicked Winnie behind him, swirling her track in patterns in the dust. He hitched her to the chapel gate and went in. He opened the tower door.

The clock struck ten. Robert knew where Father was. Every day, at ten o'clock, the time was sent from London along the telegraph wires, and the signalman opened the window of the signalbox and rang the shining bell that hung outside. And each Monday, Father went to the railway bridge and stood with his fob watch in his hand to check the time, and when the bell rang he set his watch to ten o'clock and walked down the village to the chapel to set the clock.

He was on the bridge now, waiting for that brass bell. If it rang a lot sooner or a lot later than the chapel, Father would be vexed all day. He had looked after the clock ever since he had finished being an apprentice.

The station bell rang. The clock was fast, but not much.

Robert dragged a thick square of coconut matting across the tiles and put it in the middle of the floor. There was an extending ladder hanging on the wall in the corner. Father would lift it and swing it in one move down to the mat, and push the extension up to the high platform under the roof of the first bay of the tower. Robert had often seen him do it. It was easy.

Robert took hold of the rungs, and lifted straight upwards. The ladder was heavy, but it came off its hook. Robert turned to put the ladder on the mat, but the ladder kept on turning, and took Robert with it and fell back against the wall, next to its hook. It was too heavy to lift and too heavy to put down. Robert was stuck. He turned again, and stopped as soon as the ladder moved. The ladder turned past him, but he was able to drop the end on the mat, so that it wouldn't skid.

Now Robert had the ladder in the middle of the tower, upright, wobbling, but it couldn't reach the high platform without its extension. The extension slid over the bottom half of the ladder and its own weight on hooks kept it clamped to the rungs.

Robert got his shoulder to the ladder, his legs either side of it, and lifted the extension off its first rung. The extension slid upwards, past two more rungs. Robert's grip trembled. The ladder began to lean, and with its leaning it was heavier all at once, too heavy, and the hooks were between rungs and he couldn't lock them. The ladder fell away from him, and the extension bent like a stalk.

Robert was losing his strength, as he had with the jackacre stone on the hill.

He bent and pushed again, and stuck. He felt as though he had no muscles, only a hot sharp ache, and a sharp sweet taste in his mouth. He let the hooks down on the rung. The ladder was safe; firm against the matting. It wouldn't skid. The top of the ladder was at the high platform.

Robert held the baggin cloth between his teeth, and climbed. It was a whippy ladder and it bounced under him.

From the platform there was a fixed set of steps, with iron handrails, to a trapdoor in the ceiling. The trap was lashed to a tread. Robert undid the lashing and pushed with his fingers. The trap opened, as if somebody was in the bay above, lifting. But the door had been counterweighted by Father with sashcord and bricks.

Robert went into the second bay of the tower.

Here the clock did not tick. From the road, the gentle noise could be heard, but in the second bay the pendulum swung its arc, and the clock spoke. It spoke with the same beat, but no whispered tick. The whole dark bay was the sound. Sunlight criss-crossed the floor through stained glass with marks like coloured chalks, and the air above thudded the pendulum.

A twenty-nine stave ladder led to the clock chamber above. The ladder had its own rhythm, no whip or bend, no clattering extension.

Robert always stopped to watch when he was on the ladder. The pendulum came and went in the dim light, came and went. Through the trapdoor and past the plat-

form the floor tiles were a long way off.

He climbed up, stepped sideways from the ladder to the planks of the chamber and put the baggin against the clock.

Here, everything was different again, and open. The clock case was like a hen coop, covered with tarred felt, and out of holes in the roof and sides rods connected the gears of its four faces, wires ran over pulleys to the weights that drove the clock, and a chain held the striker of the bell.

The slanted louvres filled each wall, and Robert could see the village, across to the station and Saint Philip's church. Saint Philip's had a gilded weathercock, but nothing that could tell the time. The wind and hours in Chorley were at different ends.

Robert watched the hands move on the faces of the clock. The faces held white glass in metal frames, and Father had made the hands. From inside the chamber the time was back to front.

Robert wedged himself up the wall and

reached for the cross-beam that held the frame of the clock. He hung, pulled, swung one leg over, then the other, and sat on top of the beam. He squirmed along the beam, close under the chamber roof. There was a small hatch in the roof, without hinges. He pushed at it, and it lifted and dropped back hard. It was heavy for a small square of wood. He tried again, lifting with his shoulders, and the hatch opened enough for him to jam his elbow through, then his arm, and to work the hatch sideways and clear.

Above him was darkness. But it wasn't quiet. He listened to the sound. It was no sound of clocks or of anything made. It was as if the wind had a voice and was flying in the steeple. The sound moved, never still, and under the sound was a high roaring.

Robert lifted himself on his arms through the hatchway, his legs clear of the beam. He rolled backwards and was in. He lifted the hatch, biting his lip with the heaviness, and settled it in its place. He moved gently over the floor to the wall of the steeple and sat down, hugging his knees.

The floor was smooth, covered with lead. There was lead on the hatch, and that was the weight. Robert sat in the darkness and listened to the voices above him.

It was his special place. No one else came here, to the lead-floored room in the pinnacle. No one else heard the sound.

He sat and waited for the sweeping in the air to clear. It softened, was quiet, then still. It was not all dark in the steeple. There were holes, crockets of decoration on the spire, and through them came enough light for him to see.

The room rose to a point far above, to the very capstone, and an iron bar came down through the capstone to a short beam that spanned the walls, and the bar was bolted through the beam.

A ladder went up to the beam. And on the ladder, the beam and every rough stone and brick end there were pigeons. They had flown when the hatch moved, but now the last of them was settling back, or hovering under the crockets. That had been the sound.

Beam, ladder and floor were white with droppings. It was Robert's secret cave in the air, which only pigeons knew. But the soft floor was covered with footprints, shoes and clogs and boots of every size, covered and filled with droppings, as though all the children from the village and the Moss and the Hough played here. But Robert was every one. It had been his room and place for years, and nobody knew.

Robert stood up. "Cush-cush," he said. "Cush-a-cush." The pigeons watched him, but didn't fly. He took a step on the floor, and paused, another, to the ladder. He put his hand out for a rung. A pigeon dabbed at him with its beak, but he didn't flinch. "Cush-cush." He took hold of another rung and set his weight on the ladder. "Cush-

cush. Cush-a-cush." A pigeon fluttered, and above him he heard others go. He held still until they were still. Then he began again.

In the high cave of the pinnacle Robert climbed the ladder of birds. Sometimes their voices and wings would swirl, brushing him, making shadows in shadows, and he would stop until the ladder was quiet again. Then he would climb, careful with feet and hands to ease between the birds. And the birds made space for him.

The wall closed. He could see every facet of the spire tapering around. Through the crockets there were small pictures of land. He climbed.

Robert came to the beam. From the ladder he grasped the capstone iron and stepped onto the beam. It was slippery with droppings. Below him the white ladder rustled.

"Cush-cush. Cush-a-cush," said Robert.

He looked up into the black point. Some

of the stone showed. He stretched, and reached on tip-toe to see if he had grown. He hadn't. The iron bar was long.

In all his secret, the capstone was the only part that Robert couldn't reach.

He felt the bar. It was rusty, but not sharp. And it was thick. Robert spat on his hands and took hold. He hitched himself off the beam, drew his knees up and gripped the bar with his feet. The rust held him. He stretched hand over hand, brought up his feet, gripped, hand over hand, feet; gripped. He was there. His head fitted under the capstone and his shoulders filled the spire.

Robert looked down at the birds.

The inside of the spire was rough. He put out one hand and found a hold to push against. He found another. He pressed his head to the capstone. He was firm.

Arms out, head up, Robert uncrossed his feet and let them hang. He was wearing the steeple. It fitted like a hat. He was wearing the steeple all the way to the earth, a stone dunce's cap.

"Dunce, dunce, double-D,
Can't learn his ABC!"

Robert sang, and waved his legs.

The ladder fluttered. He stopped. He took hold of the bar, and found nooks for his feet. There was nothing else.

There was nothing else. His own and private place was only this, and he felt it leave him. In all the years, there had been the last part waiting. Now he was there, and he was alone all at once, high above beam, birds, clock and no more secrets.

Robert scratched the stone with his finger. He picked at mortar and it fell. Some birds went out through the crockets. He put the flat of his hand on the top course, banged it: and stopped. He couldn't see, but his hand could feel. There was a mark on the stone, cut deep. His fingers fitted. It was a mark like an arrow. He tried to see, but there wasn't enough light.

Robert nudged his head to be more comfortable against the capstone, and felt again. It was an arrow cut into stone dressed smooth as Faddock Allman's jack-acre rocks. Robert's hand was against his face, and he walked his fingers along the course.

Right at the top of the spire, where no one could tell, the stone had been worked. Something had mattered. There was no rough rag, patched with brick. The stone was true though it would never be seen.

Robert's fingers touched a mark. It was cut as deep as the arrow, but was straight and round lines together. It was writing. Real writing. And Robert shouted so that all the birds winged and filled the steeple and beat around him. His hands were reading over and over the carved letters, over and over they read his own name.

Robert slid down the bar to beam and ladder, clattered down among buffeting wings and fear. He took no care. The droppings were slime.

He jumped his own height from the ladder

to the floor and shoved the hatch open, fell through to the cross-beam of the clock, rolled, hung, let go and landed on the edge of the platform.

"By heck!" Father had been oiling the clock, but he banged the case shut against the dust and feathers that came down with Robert. "What are you at?"

Robert ran round to the other side of the clock.

"And what have you been rolling in?" said Father. "Your mother'll play the dickens. By heck! Don't come no nearer. We could take a nest of wasps with you!"

"There's been someone up there," said Robert.

"Never," said Father. "Only you's daft enough."

"And they've carved me name," said Robert. "My name! Me own full name. Why?"

"Where's this?" said Father.

"Up top," said Robert. "Right under

the capstone."

"What do you mean, 'your' name?" said Father.

"Me name. My name. Spelt proper," said Robert.

"Oh," said Father. "And I'll lay you a wager it was beautifully done, too."

"I felt it," said Robert. "My name."

"And every inch of stone smooth as butter," said Father. "By God, ay."

"Was it you?" said Robert.

"Me?" said Father. "No, youth. That must've been cut fifty-three years or more."

"But me name!" said Robert.

"It's not your name," said Father. "It's my grandfather's. Ay. Old Robert. He was a proud, bazzil-arsed devil. But he was a good un."

Robert came from behind the clock. Father sat down on his heel and opened the baggin.

"I knew he'd capped the steeple, same as he did at Saint Philip's. But I didn't ever know him to put his name to anything. His mark, yes: never his name. Happen it mattered."

"There was a mark," said Robert. "An arrow."

"That's him," said Father. "Now you'll see his mark all over. But you have to look. He was a beggar, and he did like to tease. Well, well."

"And am I called after him?" said Robert.

"Ay, but not to much purpose yet, seemingly," said Father. He ate an onion.

"He was everywhere, all over," said Father. "But I got aback of him. A smith's aback of everyone, you see. You can't make nothing without you've a smith for your tools. But I don't know what there is for you to get aback of, youth."

"I'm going up top again," said Robert.

"Well, see as you close that hatch," said Father. "I want no feathers in me baggin, nor in the clock, neither."

Robert climbed back into the pinnacle, and closed the hatch. The birds had nearly all left the steeple in fright. A few fluttered, no longer knowing him.

His secret room for years. And, at the top, a secret. Robert took hold of the ladder.

He reached the beam, the bar, and up. When his head touched the capstone he found good bracing for his feet, and let his hands lie on the top course of stone.

In the dark his hands could read. And in the dark his hands could hear. There was a long sound in the stone. It was no sound unless Robert heard it, and meant nothing unless he gave it meaning. His chosen place had chosen him. Its end was the beginning.

Robert went down, slowly. He was gentle with the hatch. Father had the clock open and was oiling it.

"That's put a quietness on you," he said.

"Ay."

"What is it most?" said Father.

"He knew it wouldn't be seen," said

Robert. "But he did it good as any."

"Ay," said Father.

The clock hung in an iron frame. It was all rods cogs and wheels. It kept time twice. There was a drive to the hours and minutes and the pendulum, and a drive to the bell hammer. The bell was fixed, and the hour was struck on it. Both drives were weights held by two cables, each wound to a drum. The weights fitted in slots that ran down to the base of the tower.

Every week Father cleaned and oiled the clock, and wound the weights back up. It took them a week to drop the height of the tower. He wound the cables with a key like a crank handle.

"She's getting two minutes," said Father. "It's this dry weather." He reached into the clock, among the wheels and cogs and the governor that kept all steady, and he turned a small brass plate to the right. The plate was the top of the pendulum sweeping the bay below. "Just a toucher," said Father.

He did it by feel. The rhythm of the pendulum sounded the same, but Father had made it swing a little further, a little longer, and the clock would slow to the right time, until the weather changed.

"Give us a pound on the windlass, youth," said Father.

Robert liked this part of the job. It was better than turning the mangle at home, lumpy and wet.

The drums took up the cable.

"What makes wheels go round?" said Robert.

Father looked at him from the other side of the clock, through the cogs and gears.

"You, you swedgel," said Father.

"I mean wheels," said Robert. "What makes them turn?"

"You shove them," said Father.

"But why do they go round?" said Robert.

"Come here," said Father. "This side."

Robert left the winding.

"Now see at these; these wheels here," said Father. "All different sorts and sizes, aren't they, and all act according to each other?"

"Ay," said Robert.

"And if that little un there should stop, so would that big un yonder. It's all according, do you see?"

"Ay."

"Well, now," said Father, "have you ever asked yourself what makes this clock go? Have you the foggiest idea?"

Robert shook his head.

"It's this wheel," said Father. "It's the escapement."

In the middle of the clock there was a brass wheel, with pegs set on the rim of the face. Two iron teeth rocked in and out from either side by turns, holding and releasing the pegs, and the wheel came round. The teeth on the pegs were the tick of the clock.

"You wouldn't think so small a thing could make so great a sound," said Father.

"But that's escapement. And the tick goes into the pendulum. You couldn't have time without you had escapement."

"Could you not?" said Robert.

"That weight you're winding must try to get back to the ground, mustn't it?" said Father. "So it's pulling on that cable. And the cable turns the wheels. But them teeth, see at them. That comes in and catches the peg, and stops the wheel, stops the whole clock: but the pendulum's swinging, see, and in comes the other and pushes the peg forwards, and out pops the other tooth, and the pendulum swings, and back comes the tooth. Stop. Start. Day and night, for evermore: regular. It's the escapement."

"I only asked why wheels go round," said Robert.

"And I'm telling you. It's escapement," said Father. "Why do you think them weights drop at all? You could say as you weren't winding weights up, you were winding chapel down. It comes to the same. It's all according, gears and cogs. We're going at that much of a rattle, the whole blooming earth, moon and stars, we need escapement to hold us together.''

"I must go help me Uncle Charlie," said Robert, and stepped onto the ladder, into the pendulum bay.

"That's right," said Father. "I knew I could've saved me breath."

Robert went.

"By, it's a day's work to watch you put the kettle on," said Father.

Robert went.

"Hey!" Father called after him.

"What?" said Robert.

"Was it you as took the extension off the wall and reared it up?"

"Ay!"

"By yourself?"

"Ay!"

"You're shaping, youth," said Father.

Robert untied Wicked Winnie, and ran with her along the road. "What's he on at?"

he said. " 'Escapement'? That's not escapement. It's fine oil."

He was able to ride a little under the wood, but he had to keep running to push.

"Who-whoop! Wo-whoop! Wo-o-o-o!"

Robert heard the distant cry of the summer fields go up on Leah's Hill.

"Who-whoop! Wo-whoop! Wo-o-o-o!"

The men were excited. "Who-whoop! Wo-whoop! Wo-o-o-o! Who-whoop! Wo-whoop! Wo-o-o-o!"

Then Robert heard a shot. It was hard, not like a gun. There was another. And four quickly after that. And silence. Robert listened. There was no sound. The heat was pressing the day flat, and the air thick with it.

Robert left Wicked Winnie at the gate and ran into the house. He could hear Mother making the beds.

"Father's fettling the clock!" he called up the bent stairs. "I'm off up Leah's!"

But first Robert cleaned Wicked Winnie

again, and rubbed linseed into her wood. Then he put the kettle on the fire for Faddock Allman's brew, and went out.

The bottom field was cut, neat with kivvers. The men and women were eating their food under the hedge. Uncle Charlie was leaving for the road. He had his rifle slung on one shoulder and Faddock Allman over the other.

"Dick-Richard! I want you!" he shouted.

"What for?" said Robert.

"Never mind what for. Let's be having you. The tooter the sweeter."

Robert ran to where Uncle Charlie stood by the gate.

"Gently does it, Starie Chelevek," said Uncle Charlie. And he carefully set Faddock Allman down in Wicked Winnie.

"Where's he going?" said Robert.

"He's having his dinner with me," said Uncle Charlie.

"At our house?" said Robert.

"Where else?" said Uncle Charlie.

"Has Father said?"

"He's not been asked," said Uncle Charlie. He bent down to Faddock Allman's helmet. It had slipped over one ear.

"I'll have me brew same as usual," said Faddock Allman. "Young un fetches for me."

"Eyes front," said Uncle Charlie. "Straighten your pith pot. Get on parade, me old Toby."

"Was that you shooting?" said Robert.

"Ay," said Uncle Charlie. "I'm back at work Tuesday: so I might as good practise."

"I'll not come in," said Faddock Allman. "I'll not disturb your dinners."

They had reached the house.

"Who's having their dinners disturbed?" said Uncle Charlie.

"I'd sooner not," said Faddock Allman.

"What must I do?" said Robert.

"Bung him round the back," said Uncle Charlie. "He can sun hisself, and I'll feed him through the window."

Robert took Faddock Allman round the side of the house and put him against the white limewash, under the thatch.

"Shan't you be too hot, Mister Allman?" said Robert.

"Champion," said Faddock Allman. "Grand." He watched the sun.

Robert went back in.

"Will he be all right?" he said. "It's a whole topcoat warmer against our back wall."

"Not for that old sweat," said Uncle Charlie. "He did his soldiering in Mesopolonica. He's used to it."

Uncle Charlie lifted the boiling kettle off the fire and made a brew of cocoa. He took the brew, the kettle and his rifle with him into the garden.

"Warm enough?" he said.

"Grand," said Faddock Allman.

Uncle Charlie gave him his brew. Then he cleaned his rifle. He put the bolt and the magazine on one side and poured the boiling water down the barrel, the whole five pint kettle.

He looked into the barrel from both ends, and pulled a length of rag through, fastened to a cord, time and time again until the rifle was dry. He picked up his oil bottle; and frowned.

"Who's had this?" he said. "Some beggar's touched this."

"It was me," said Robert.

"And who gave you permission?" said Uncle Charlie.

"It wasn't more than a drop," said Robert. "I needed it for her wheels."

"I don't care what you need," said Uncle Charlie. "And you don't touch, think on."

He oiled the moving parts of the gun, the catches, magazine, levers, bolt and barrel.

Father came round the corner of the house. He had put his bicycle against the gable end. He stopped when he saw Faddock Allman.

"Now then, Faddock," said Father.

"Now then, Joseph," said Uncle Charlie.

Faddock Allman drank his brew and said nothing. Father looked at Uncle Charlie and went inside.

"Put the kettle on, Dick-Richard," said Uncle Charlie.

Robert filled the kettle, and took it to the fire. Mother was serving Father his dinner. Robert ran back again quickly.

Uncle Charlie had assembled his rifle and was rattling the breech open and closed.

"Ease! Springs!" shouted Faddock Allman.

Father shut the window from inside.

Uncle Charlie smiled. "We're a right pair, aren't we, Dick-Richard? Your father and me? Him sitting up in that chapel, like a great barn owl, oiling his clock. And me, oiling this. Eh?"

Robert pointed to a bent piece of metal on the rifle. "Is that the escapement?" he said.

"The eswhatment?" said Uncle Charlie.

"That's the cocking piece locking re-sistence."

"Oh," said Robert.

"I'd best be doing," said Faddock Allman. "Now as Master's having his dinner."

"You stand easy, Starie Chelevek," said Uncle Charlie. "I'll fetch you some dinner meself."

"No. I'll be off. Young un takes me," said Faddock Allman.

"Does he?" said Uncle Charlie. He picked up Wicked Winnie's sashcord and put two turns of it around the boot scraper by the door and pulled all his weight on the knot. "Let him unfasten that, then. Come on, Dick-Richard. There's top field to be cut this after."

He took his rifle and Robert into the house and sat at the table, on the sofa by the window. Father was eating. Robert stood near the door. Mother poured fresh tea.

"It's not brewed," said Father.

"It's wet," said Uncle Charlie.

"Why isn't this tea brewed?" said Father.

"By, it's close in here, isn't it, Joseph?" said Uncle Charlie, and opened the window. Father leaned across and shut it.

"Give over," said Uncle Charlie. "I've been second man to Ozzie Leah on the scythe all morning, and I could do with a drop of coolth."

Father tapped the table with his square-ended fingers as he spoke. "What's yon Mossaggot think he's doing here while I'm having me dinner?" he said.

"I fetched him. I'm feeding him," said Uncle Charlie.

"There's a war on," said Father.

"Eh up! Where?" said Uncle Charlie. "Now, Joseph: Charlie's home. Joseph, whenever has the stockpot gone short when Charlie's home, eh? There's good flesh-meat, isn't there, and without granching your teeth on lead shot? Come on, Joseph. Charlie's home."

He put his hand on Father's arm. His own arm was thin and brown under the golden hairs. Father looked down at the arm.

"Get off with your mithering," said Father. He ate angrily.

"I seem to recollect, Joseph," said Uncle Charlie, "as how it hadn't used to matter so much when Faddock Allman was being shot to beggary by them Boers."

Father didn't answer. Uncle Charlie cut a round of bread, spread it with dripping, and opened the window. "Cop hold," he said to Faddock Allman, and left the window open.

"Eh, Dick-Richard," said Uncle Charlie. "Your father's vexed, seemingly. What must we do to cheer him up?"

Robert looked quickly at Father, and caught a flash of blue eye. Robert said nothing.

"Here, Dick-Richard," said Uncle Charlie. "Over here."

Robert went. Father ate. Robert was ready to run.

But Uncle Charlie was quicker. He grabbed Robert with both hands, and lifted him and stood him on the table. Robert's boots clattered among the dishes and his head touched the ceiling beams. He was looking into both men's eyes.

"Give us a song, Dick-Richard," said Uncle Charlie. "One for to win a war with, eh? A penny. See." He pulled a penny out of his pocket and slid it on the table, holding it under his finger. Robert looked at Father again, but Father was eating.

Robert's boots shuffled the tea pot. He felt Uncle Charlie's hand firm holding to his britches. So he sang.

> "*Kitchener's Army,*
> *Working all day,*
> *What does he pay them?*
> *A shilling a day.*
> *What if they grumble?*
> *The Colonel will say,*

'Put them in the guardroom,
And stop all their pay'."

Uncle Charlie hefted Robert down by his britches, and pushed the penny towards him.

Robert took the penny. Father still ate.

"Dear, dear, Joseph," said Uncle Charlie. "Will music never sooth the savage breast? What else can we do?"

He took the bolt and magazine out of his rifle, squinted down the barrel, and put it to his lips as if it were a trumpet. He blew a note.

"Just tuning," said Uncle Charlie. "No harm done."

He blew again, and, by altering the shape of his lips, he played the notes of "Abide With Me". His face was dark red and his eyes rolled.

"You daft ha'porth!" Father nearly choked on his food. Uncle Charlie tried to wink at Robert, and went on playing. "You

lommering, gawming, kay-pawed gowf!"
shouted Father, and coughed and laughed
his dinner over the table. "Give over! Any
allsorts can play that dirge! Let's have some
triple-tonguing!"

"What tune must I play?" said Uncle
Charlie.

"There's not but one tune," said Father.
He opened the corner cupboard and took
out his own E Flat cornet. "There's not but
one tune." He wet his lips, loosened the
valves of the cornet, and looked at Robert.
"I'll give you the note, youth. But you can
stay off the table. Right!"

Father and Uncle Charlie drew in breath
together, and Father began the great tune of
the Hough, triple-tongued, fast. Uncle
Charlie hit what notes he could, and Robert
sang to the soprano E Flat.

> *"Oh, can you wash a soldier's shirt?*
> *And can you wash it clean?*
> *Oh, can you wash a soldier's shirt,*
> *And hang it on the green?"*

"And again!" shouted Father. "Ready!"

"Retreat! Forward! Charge!" shouted Faddock Allman beneath the window.

Robert couldn't sing. His neck hurt. Uncle Charlie slid under the table with laughing. And Father played, his cap on his head, standing above his dinner, and played until the tune was finished.

"Ay," said Father. "Mesopolonica."

After dinner, Robert took Faddock Allman back to the stones by the roadside. Uncle Charlie walked with him, carrying his rifle and a spade from the end room of the house.

"Your father," said Uncle Charlie. "Take no notice. He was a bit upset."

"I know," said Robert.

"He's a man very fluent in giving."

"I know."

"It's them horseshoes and the hours," said Uncle Charlie. "They could take his touch away for ever, him as is the only best smith from Chorley to Mottram. If I was Joseph, I reckon I'd live in chapel clock till this lot was done with. But I'm lucky, Dick-Richard. It's me trade. Now. What shall you be?"

Uncle Charlie lifted Faddock Allman onto his sacking and gave him the hammers, and the rifle.

"I've not thought," said Robert.

"Well, what do you want?"

"All in!" shouted Ozzie Leah.

The men and women moved to the top field.

"What do you want?" Uncle Charlie said again.

Robert went with him, pulling Wicked Winnie, up the hill towards the jackacre patch.

"I like seeing to Mister Allman," said Robert. "And getting for him."

"Good God, youth, that's no trade!" said Uncle Charlie. "You want craft and masterness in you! You're no Mossaggot! You're a Houghite! You must have a trade!"

"Can I work with you, then?" said Robert.

Uncle Charlie picked up his scythe and gave the spade to Robert.

"I work by meself," he said. "I've no apprentices."

"Have you not?" said Robert.

"No, I haven't," said Uncle Charlie.

"I can be a soldier if I want," said Robert.

"And why do you want?" said Uncle Charlie.

"The marching and that," said Robert. "And they give you medals, same as you and Mister Allman."

"Your father calls them bits stuck on the outside of one chap for sticking bits on the inside of another," said Uncle Charlie. "And he's right. No, youth. You must have the flavour for soldiering. I've got it, and you haven't. It's not in you. Now then: here's your next fatigue."

They were at the jackacre patch. It was a

sandhole with stones, ragged at the edge from Robert's morning.

"You can fill this lot in," said Uncle Charlie, "and grass it over."

"I'll not fill that in!" said Robert. "There's ever so many stones come out."

"No," said Uncle Charlie, "but you can smooth it round for Ozzie Leah to lead his cart in for the kivvers when they've stood. He'd break an axle, the way you've got it now."

Ozzie Leah, Uncle Charlie and Young Ollie took their stand in the field. The scythes lifted and the swarfs fell. Round the field they went. The sun shone.

Robert tried to level the hole. It was a lonely, hot job, dull, not like the morning when everything was being found. He shovelled and sweated, patched the ground with turf and trod it in.

The sun was so hot that it took all colour from the land.

"Whet!" shouted Ozzie.

Everywhere but the corn was black and dark green. Saint Philip's church was black, its weathervane cockerel black and just proud of the horizon. The whole land lacked shadows or relief, but for the corn and a bloom of light on the tops of the beech trees in the wood above Long Croft.

They worked the afternoon.

"Whet!" shouted Ozzie.

Kivvers and stubble followed the men, round and round, the square spiral tightened on the field.

At baggin time Uncle Charlie came down to see how Robert had managed. He looked at the grass and earth.

"I said smooth it, youth, not build a flipping parapet."

"Well, cob you!" shouted Robert. "Cob you, then!"

And he stuck his spade in the ground and ran down the field to Faddock Allman. Uncle Charlie followed with the beer. He was smiling. Robert lay under the hedge, batting at flies with his hands.

Faddock Allman and Uncle Charlie drank, and Uncle Charlie passed the stone jar to Robert. "There's more to feckazing than feckazing, isn't there, youth?" he said.

"It's these clegs," said Robert. "They're eating me."

"Clegs don't bite," said Uncle Charlie. "They've got hot feet."

The sweat dried.

"But, without you've a trade, feckazing is all you'll get," said Uncle Charlie.

"I want more stone," said Faddock Allman.

"Then you can want," said Uncle Charlie, and polished the stock of his rifle.

"Where are you working?" said Robert.

"Oh, all over," said Uncle Charlie. "Wherever there's call. Plug Street, mostly."

"Where's that?" said Robert.

"Aback of Leah's Hill," said Uncle Charlie.

"How do you get there?" said Robert.

"Train. Then boat. It costs nowt. The King pays. Then another train. Then you walk it. Past Dicky Bush and Roody Boys, over Hazy Brook, till you come to Funky Villas. Turn left for Moo-Cow Farm, and Plug Street's second on the right."

"You're twitting me," said Robert.

"But that's where I'll be working, Tuesday," said Uncle Charlie. "Plug Street."

"Is it a journey?" said Robert.

"It is when you're carrying full pack," said Uncle Charlie. "But I reckon I'll go a shorter way, meself. I reckon I just about shall. I might just go the aimer gate this time. I've done enough traipsing."

"All in!" shouted Ozzie Leah.

Uncle Charlie and Robert went back up the field. It was still hot, but the sun was redder.

Robert took all the turf off the jackacre and curved its line and shallowed it. Then he put the turf back. He watched the reapers. They moved more gentle than the chapel clock.

"Whet!" shouted Ozzie.

There was a square of corn uncut in the middle of the field. Ozzie and Young Ollie sharpened up, but Uncle Charlie came down to the corner by the gate where Robert was, and laid his scythe against the hedge.

Robert pointed to the jackacre. "Will it do?" he said.

"Ay. It'll do," said Uncle Charlie. "Now fetch Faddock Allman and me rifle."

Robert went down the hill on Wicked Winnie, using his heels.

"Mister Allman," he said, "me Uncle Charlie wants you, and we're to take him his rifle."

Faddock Allman swung himself into Wicked Winnie and picked up the rifle wrapped in sacking. "All present and correct!" he shouted. "Mount!"

Robert put the sashcord across his shoulders and climbed the field. His boots were still slippery, and Faddock Allman was so heavy that Robert had to zig-zag along the hill. "You can go where you please, you can shin up trees," sang Faddock Allman at every turn, "but you can't get away from the guns!" Robert was sobbing with sweat by the time he reached the top field.

"Number Six-six Battery, Royal Field Artillery, ready for inspection! Sir!" shouted Faddock Allman.

Uncle Charlie didn't answer. He was on his heel, chewing a straw of stubble, and looking at the standing corn. His face had gone different. It was thinner, and Robert couldn't tell what was in the eyes. He spat the straw out and drank from a flask he carried in his pocket, enough to wet his mouth, no more.

Uncle Charlie stood up. He took the rifle. "Get aback of me," he said.

Robert made Wicked Winnie safe with chocks of stone. Faddock Allman pushed his helmet off his forehead. The men and boys were standing around the square of corn, and were silent. The women had moved away down the hill.

"Ready?" Ozzie Leah called.

Uncle Charlie nodded. He loaded the magazine with real bullets, grey iron and brass, clipped the magazine into the rifle, put another bullet in the breech and rattled the bolt. He held the rifle across his body, pointing to the earth, flexed his shoulders and breathed deeply, and then was still.

Ozzie Leah looked at Uncle Charlie once more, raised his hand, his cap in it, and brought it down.

"Who-whoop! Wo-whoop! Wo-o-o-o! Who-whoop! Wo-whoop! Wo-o-o-o!" The men and boys yelled the cry. They yelled and yelled and clapped their hands and waved their caps and banged sticks together. Uncle Charlie didn't move. "Who-whoop! Wo-whoop! Wo-o-o-o!" The noise was tremendous.

But through the noise came another, a scream, a squeal, and, in terror, rabbits broke out of the last standing corn. All day they had worked inward from the scythes, and now they ran. Uncle Charlie watched. Over the field, between the kivvers, dodging, driven by noise, the rabbits went and their screaming pierced all noise.

Uncle Charlie swung the rifle to his shoulder, turning on his hips. He fired. The sound of the rifle deadened Robert's ears. Left. Left. Right. Left. "Who-whoop! Wo-whoop! Wo-o-o-o!" Right.

One rabbit was going uphill, in line with the men. Uncle Charlie watched it go until it climbed above them. The rabbit was at the top cornerpost of the field when he shot it.

The others got away. Their squealing stopped when they reached the bracken of the wood.

And Saint Philip's church was still black, and there were no shadows.

Ozzie Leah shouted, "Good lad, Sniper!"

Robert looked at Uncle Charlie. The face was no different. "When there's too many," said Uncle Charlie, "you can't tell them from poppies. They're all alike the same, you see."

"Cop hold, Sniper," said Ozzie Leah. "Three for you, and a sixpence for the bullets." He had brought the rabbits down to Uncle Charlie. They had all been shot in the head, and none of the meat was spoilt, though the heads had gone. "Me and Ollie can finish," said Ozzie Leah. "You get off home, there's a good lad."

"Ay," said Uncle Charlie.

He took the three rabbits and the spade and the sashcord and his rifle and walked off the hill, as if Faddock Allman was leading him, like a big dog. And Robert followed.

They sat by the heap of road flint stone and gutted the rabbits. Uncle Charlie lifted his eyes to look at the work he had done, at

the harvest got.

"That's my trade, Dick-Richard," said Uncle Charlie. "I stop rabbits skriking. There's me craft, and there's my masterness."

They wiped their hands on grass. Together Robert and Uncle Charlie pulled Faddock Allman as far as the house. At the gate, Robert carried the hammers in to the end room while Uncle Charlie went to fetch Faddock Allman his brew for the night. Father was finishing supper. Mother began to skin the rabbits.

Uncle Charlie boiled out his rifle, dried it and cleaned it and took it into the kitchen. He sat down at the table.

"Now then, Joseph," said Uncle Charlie.

"Now then, Charlie," said Father.

They looked at each other, and they laughed.

The corn kivvers waited on three church bells. The last cry went up, "Who-whoop! Wo-whoop! Wo-o-o-o!" and was quiet at

Leah's Hill. Wicked Winnie took Faddock Allman home. Father and Uncle Charlie played the great tune of the Hough, E Flat cornet and rifle, on either side of the fire, and the day swung in the chapel clock, escapement to the sun.